TEAM SUPERCREW presents

GEN THE GRIT IN

I QUIT!

By **Julie Anne Penn** and **Darren Penn**   Illustrated by **Sergio De Giorgi**

For all the kids that might be scared...you can!

– J.P. and D.P.

To "little" Nano

– S.D.G

Five to One Press
www.fivetoonepress.com

Copyright 2022 by Five to One Press - New York, NY

ISBN Hardcover: 979-8-9872024-2-5   ISBN Softcover: 979-8-9854707-7-2

Library of Congress Control Number: 2022916819

First edition, 2022

Illustrator: Sergio De Giorgi
Interior and Cover Designer: Jess Lam

Printed in China

A speclal thanks to Dr. Jamie Schrager and Dr. Kristen Piering.

Team Supercrew Be Extraordinary is a trademark of Supercrew Incorporated.

www.teamsupercrew.com
info@teamsupercrew.com

WE'RE TEAM SUPERCREW! Superhero kids with awesome abilities: the power to be brave, the power to be kind, the power to be calm, and the power of grit. We help kids find their own powers when they need them most. Want to join us?

Benny the Brave   Keisha the Kind   Chloe the Calm   Gen the Grit

"Oh Gen, what's the point,
I'm not good at soccer. I quit!"

"Hey, Kiddo! Let's get ready for practice.
Don't forget your soccer ball!"

"I can't go to practice today, Gen."

"I'm...so...nervous."

"Gen! But how? Is that really, really you?"

"Of course it's me! Gen's my name and grit's my game!"

"I hear you need some help. Why are you nervous?"

I'm not sure what to do."

everyone is watching me."

"I'm nervous because...

I can't kick well."

what if I make a mistake?
I don't want to make anyone feel bad."

"Wow, this is scary!"

"It's okay to feel nervous.

But...what if..."

"You're part of a team,

you are friends, and everyone matters!"

you are loved. Everyone is there to support you and cheer you on whether you win or lose!"

"What if...

the real goal is trying your best and not giving up!"

"What if...

we get better by learning from our mistakes. Nobody's perfect!"

"What if...

I won't give up.
I'll keep trying. I do have grit!"

"Of course you do! And as a friend of Team Supercrew, you now have the power of grit inside of you."

"What if...

it's always been there."

WANT TO BUILD YOUR SUPERHERO SKILLS?

Next time you need a boost of grit, try these four simple steps:

1. Notice how you're feeling. Are you feeling anxious, overwhelmed, nervous, scared? All of these feelings are okay, and lots of kids (and adults too!) experience them all the time.

2. Share your thoughts and feelings with a trusted adult or friend.

3. Try to change your thoughts so they are more positive or hopeful. You might even think about a time before when you didn't give up and had grit. Friends and adults can help you with this part.

4. Notice how you're feeling now. Did the feeling change?

Your thoughts create your feelings! You now have the power to find your grit and not give up, just like **Gen and Jordan!**

Want to make your own Grit Book? Scan the QR code for your free Grit Book template!

TEAM SUPERCREW presents

CHLOE THE CALM IN

THE BEDTIME BLUES

By **Julie Anne Penn** and **Darren Penn**   Illustrated by **Sergio De Giorgi**

For our parents - the real superheroes
- J.P. and D.P.

For my lovely Sinan
- S.D.G

ISBN Hardcover: 979-8-9872024-1-8   ISBN Softcover: 979-8-9854707-5-8

Library of Congress Control Number: 2022914859

First edition, 2022

Illustrator: Sergio De Giorgi
Interior and Cover Designer: Jess Lam

Printed in China

A special thanks to Jamie Schrager, Psy.D. and Kristen Piering, Psy.D.

Team Supercrew Be Extraordinary is a trademark of Supercrew Incorporated.

www.teamsupercrew.com
info@teamsupercrew.com

WE'RE TEAM SUPERCREW! Superhero kids with awesome abilities: the power to be brave, the power to be kind, the power to be calm, and the power of grit. We help kids find their own powers when they need them most. Want to join us?

Benny the Brave   Keisha the Kind   Chloe the Calm   Gen the Grit

"All right, Miko. Lights out. It's time for some beautiful, amazing, wonderful dreams. You'll need your rest for the ballet recital tomorrow."

"But I'm not tired. Not even close.
Only you would understand, Chloe."

"I don't want to go to bed.

There's no way I'm going to bed right now."

"I'm...so...mad!"

"Wow!"

"Is it? Can it be? Chloe, is that you?"

"Of course it's me, Chloe the Calm."

"But hang on a minute. Let me breathe in and out.
Ah, that's so much better. I hear you need some help.
Why are you mad?"

"I'm mad because...

if I go to bed, I'll miss all the fun!"

all my friends stay up really late!"

there are so many things I want to do!"

I'm not tired!"

"It's okay to feel mad."

"But...what if...

you were calm and dreamed about
special places that belonged only to you!"

"What if...

you were calm, had a good night's sleep,
and did your best at the ballet recital!"

the real fun is knowing you can enjoy
tomorrow and not miss a thing!"

"What if...

your friends need rest, too!"

"What if...

I am calm.
I feel better already!"

"Yes, Miko. As a calm friend of Team Supercrew, you now have the power to be calm inside of you whenever you need it."

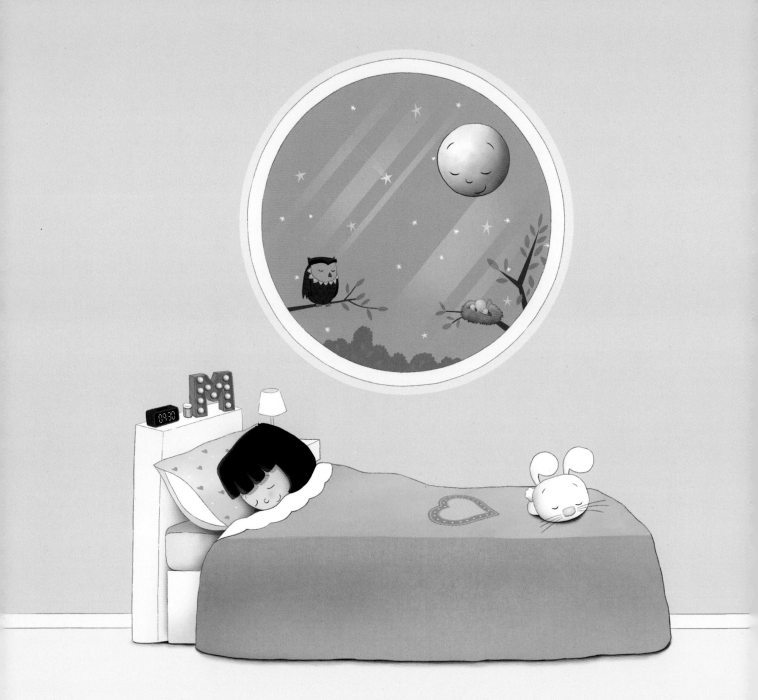

"Goodnight, Chloe."

"What if...

it's always been there."

WANT TO BUILD YOUR SUPERHERO SKILLS?

Next time you need a calm reset, try these four simple steps:

1. Notice how you're feeling. Are you feeling anxious, excited, restless, scared? All of these feelings are okay, and lots of kids (and adults, too!) experience them all the time.

2. Share your thoughts and feelings with a trusted adult or friend.

3. Try to change your thoughts so they are more positive or hopeful. You might even think about a time before when you were able to be calm. Friends and adults can help you with this part.

4. Notice how you're feeling now. Did the feeling change?

Want to make your own Calm Book? Scan the QR code for your free Calm Book template!

Your thoughts create your feelings! You now have the power to think calm thoughts and be calm whenever you need it, just like **Chloe and Miko!**

TEAM SUPERCREW presents

KEISHA THE KIND IN

MY LITTLE SISTER SITUATION

By **Julie Anne Penn** and **Darren Penn**   Illustrated by **Sergio De Giorgi**

For our little brother and big sister
– J.P. and D.P.

To Vanina, my lovely Super Sister
– S.D.G

Copyright 2022 by Five to One Press - New York, NY

All rights reserved. No part of this publication, or the characters within it, may be reproduced or distributed in any form or by any means without prior written consent of the publisher.

ISBN Hardcover: 979-8-9872024-0-1   ISBN Softcover: 979-8-9854707-2-7

Library of Congress Control Number: 2022909738

First edition, 2022

Illustrator: Sergio De Giorgi
Interior and Cover Designer: Jess Lam

Printed in China

A speclal thanks to Jamie Schrager, Psy.D., Kristen Piering, Psy.D., Jason Craig Harris, Tomiko Fraser Hines, Vanessa De Riggs, and Erin Williams.

Team Supercrew Be Extraordinary is a trademark of Supercrew Incorporated.

www.teamsupercrew.com
info@teamsupercrew.com

WE'RE TEAM SUPERCREW! Superhero kids with awesome abilities: the power to be kind, the power to be brave, the power of grit, and the power to be calm. We help kids find their own powers when they need them most. Want to join us?

Benny the Brave   Keisha the Kind   Chloe the Calm   Gen the Grit

"Hey, Danny. I'm going downstairs to make breakfast.
Can you watch your sister for a few minutes?"

"Oh, Keisha. I wish you were here."

"I'm...so...frustrated."

"Wow, what's happening?"

"Keisha, is it you? Can it be? But...how?"

"You called me and I came!"

"As a proud member of Team Supercrew, I, Keisha
the Kind am here to help. Why are you frustrated?"

my sister always takes my toys!"

"I feel frustrated because...

she always wants to play the things I don't like."

"I feel frustrated because...

she's always wrecking my stuff."

she gets all the attention."

"Wow, that does sound frustrating!"

"It's okay to feel frustrated."

"But...what if...

your sister loves to play with your toys,
because they remind her of you!"

"What if...

you were once an explorer like your sister, finding your
way in the world with wide eyes and endless curiosity!"

a big brother leads by example."

you are your sister's hero."

"Of course you are! You're a great big brother, too. As a kind friend of Team Supercrew, you now have the power inside of you whenever you need it."

"What if...

it's always been there."

WANT TO BUILD YOUR SUPERHERO SKILLS?

Next time you need a kindness boost, try these four simple steps:

Kindness is about being gentle with ourselves as well as others. Here are some ways we can be kind:

1. Notice how you are feeling. Are you feeling frustrated? Angry? Sad? All of these feelings are okay and lots of kids (and adults, too!) experience them all the time.

2. Share your thoughts and feelings with a trusted adult or friend.

3. Try to change your thoughts so they are more positive or hopeful. You may even think about a time you showed kindness to yourself and others before. Friends and adults can help you with this part.

4. Notice how you're feeling now.

Your thoughts create your feelings. You now have the power to think kind thoughts and show kindness whenever you need it, just like **Keisha and Danny!**

Want to make your own Kind Book? Scan the QR code for your free Kind Book template!

TEAM **SUPERCREW** presents

BENNY THE BRAVE IN

THE FIRST DAY JITTERS

By **Julie Anne Penn** and **Darren Penn**   Illustrated by **Sergio De Giorgi**

For BB...our greatest teacher
- J.P. and D.P.

For April, Emma, and Vivi—my superheroes
- S.D.G

ISBN Hardcover: 979-8-9854707-9-6   ISBN Softcover: 979-8-9854707-0-3

Library of Congress Control Number: 2022906637

First edition, 2022

Cover Designer: Jess Lam
Editor: Lauren Kerstein

Printed in China

A special thanks to Jamie Schrager, Psy.D., Kristen Piering, Psy.D., Amanda Lupis, Kimberley Mauro, Ella, Jack, and Felix.

Team Supercrew Be Extraordinary is a trademark of Supercrew Incorporated.

www.teamsupercrew.com
info@teamsupercrew.com

WE'RE TEAM SUPERCREW! Superhero kids with awesome abilities: the power to be kind, the power to be brave, the power of grit, and the power to be calm. We help kids find their own powers when they need them most. Want to join us?

Benny the Brave   Keisha the Kind   Chloe the Calm   Gen the Grit

"I don't want to go to school today."

"It's my first day, Benny."

"The bus will be here in five minutes, Honey.
I'll meet you by the front door, lickety-split!"

"Oh, Benny. I wish you could come with me."

"I...am...scared."

"What's happening?"

"Whoa! Benny. What? How...? I must be dreaming."

"Hey, Sarah. Did you say you're scared?"

"You called me and I came! As a proud member of
Team Supercrew, I, Benny the Brave am here to help.
Why are you scared?"

my new school is so far away."

2 + 3 = 5
4 − 2 = 2
6 − 5 = 1

my teacher will have gigantic
teeth and a long, slimy tail."

my lunch will be squirmy and squishy and gross!"

"I feel scared because...

I am new and nobody will want to play with me."

"It's okay to feel scared.

But...what if..."

"You love adventures!"

Mr. Tom has a pet turtle just like you!"

"What if...

Mom packed your favorite cheese sandwich. And look, a chocolate-chip cookie. The big one!"

"What if...

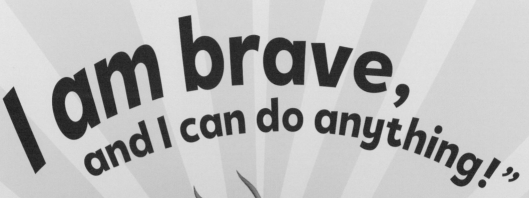

"What if...

I am brave,
and I can do anything!"

"Yes! You are brave and you can do anything!
As a brave friend of Team Supercrew, you now have
the power inside of you whenever you need it."

"Coming Mom!"

"I'll be right there!"

"What if...

It's always been there."

WANT TO BUILD YOUR SUPERHERO SKILLS?

Next time you need a bravery boost, try these four simple steps:

1. Notice how you're feeling. Are you feeling scared? Worried? Nervous? Lonely? All of these feelings are okay, and lots of kids (and adults, too!) experience them all the time.

2. Share your thoughts and feelings with a trusted adult or friend.

3. Try to change your thoughts so they are more positive or hopeful. You might even think about a time you showed bravery before. Friends and adults can help you with this part.

4. Notice how you're feeling now. Did the feeling change?

Your thoughts create your feelings! You now have the power to think brave thoughts and show bravery whenever you need it, just like **Benny and Sarah!**

Want to make your own Brave Book? Scan the QR code for your free Brave Book template!